Original story by Alain Grée, illustrated by Luis Camps
Translated by Gillian M. Goslinga

# Wally the Woodpecker

## Frog Pond Friends

Derrydale Books

New York

**W**ally the woodpecker is always helping his Frog Pond Friends in the forest. First he chops down a branch for Ronnie the rabbit. Then he hollows the trunk of a pine tree for Sammy the squirrel. And there he is again, carving the bark of an oak tree into a board for Ricky the raccoon! Wally is so clever with his beak! To thank the hard working woodpecker, the Frog Pond Friends invite him to share lunch with them. Though woodpeckers love more than anything to peck at wood, they never refuse to peck at tasty food!

But this morning Wally is not in a very good mood. Worse than that, he refuses to peck at the smallest twig! "Unbelievable!" declares Flap the frog. "Since he's started to read that book, nothing else interests him!" Barbie the bee cups her ears to listen. "Quiet now! He is reading aloud..." "Protect nature," reads Wally without even looking up at his friends. "Trees, like all other vegetation, are living beings. They are born and they grow with age. One must not hurt them unnecessarily..."

Harry the hedgehog is worried. "If Wally doesn't want to help us anymore, what will we do when we need to fix our homes for the winter months?" "I could chew on a few branches," proposes Benjamin the beaver. "But Wally works so much faster and better!" "That's true," says Danny the dog, sadly shaking his head. "He knows how to carve the walls of my doghouse perfectly!"

"And each honeycomb in my beehive..." adds Barbie with a sigh.

"Wally is right," adds Ollie the owl. "Our duty is to protect nature. But one can trim a plant without hurting it. And isn't the lawn greener after it has been mowed?" "Of course!" answers Charlotte the turtle. "But our problem is this—Wally's head is as hard as his beak! No one will ever make him change his mind!" Bernie the bear jumps on top of an old trunk. "He needs to change his mind himself," he explains. "And I think with the help of these theater props we can make him do that."

Bernie rummages through his trunk. "Here he comes! Quick! Put on these wigs!" When Wally sees his friends with long hair and beards, he is dumbfounded. "Wally," Bernie starts without smiling, "we have come to the serious conclusion that one should not restrict nature in any way. We therefore have decided to never cut our hair or beards or nails again!"

PROTECT NATURE

PRO NA

Ricky continues, "By the way, Wally, would you have given up protecting nature by any chance?" "Of course not!" replies the woodpecker. "But I am very hungry! Since I stopped nibbling on branches, I can't find the tiniest ant to eat! Could you spare a fish, Ricky?" The raccoon sadly glances at his empty scoop-net. "Unfortunately, I haven't caught a single fish since I let my hair grow long!"

Disappointed, Wally turns to Mrs. Rabbit. "Mrs. Rabbit, you make such delicious cakes. Could you give me a slice?" "Unfortunately," says Mrs. Rabbit, "there is no wheat to buy!" "But the wheat fields look so ripe. . ." says Wally, surprised. "That's true, they have never been so golden. But the farmer refuses to harvest the wheat. He is too afraid to hurt nature!"

Will his friend Barbie the bee be more generous? "And you Barbie, are you going to refuse me a spoonful of honey? A little spoonful of honey. . ." begs Wally, starved. Barbie flapped her wings. "Unfortunately, I no longer collect pollen. I am too afraid of scratching the flowers as I land on them!" she explains. "And without any pollen, there can be no honey!" adds Danny the dog, winking sideways at his friends. "What can we do, Wally, we either must eat or protect nature. . ."

PROTECT NATURE

FOR SALE

A few lumberjacks are working nearby in the forest. "But...you cut trees!" cries Wally, shocked. "My book says we should protect them..." "Your book is right," says the forest ranger, smiling, "no plant is as precious as a tree. And it's to help the forest breathe and the trees grow stronger that we come and cut a few branches here and there or chop down a few tree trunks."